JOURNEY TO THE WEST

WU CHENG'EN

www.realreads.co.uk

Retold by Christine Sun
Illustrated by Shirley Chiang

Published by Real Reads Ltd
Stroud, Gloucestershire, UK
www.realreads.co.uk

First published in 2011
Reprinted 2013, 2014 (twice), 2016

ISBN 978-1-906230-34-0

Printed in China by Wai Man Book Binding (China) Ltd
Designed by Lucy Guenot
Typeset by Bookcraft Ltd, Stroud, Gloucestershire

CONTENTS

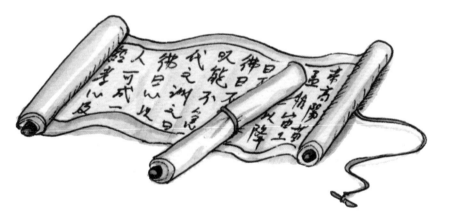

THE CHARACTERS

Monkey

Monkey is clever and courageous, but can he change his mischievous ways and become the loyal disciple of his master Xuanzang?

Xuanzang

Xuanzang is a handsome monk, travelling to India to find the precious scriptures. Will he survive the dangerous journey and the monsters who want to eat him?

Piggy

Piggy is a happy-go-lucky pig who enjoys drinking and pursuing beautiful women. Can he overcome these habits and look after his master Xuanzang?

Sandy

Sandy is an ogre, but he is a talented fighter, especially underwater. Will he be able to handle the challenges that threaten to destroy his faith?

Buddha and Guanyin

Two of the many deities who watch over the world and guide those in need to their salvation. Can they help Xuanzang and his disciples find their way?

Buffalo King, Red Boy, and Princess Iron-Fan

Three of the many monsters and demons who try to eat Xuanzang on his journey. What are their cunning plans and secret magical weapons?

JOURNEY TO THE WEST

Bang!

A very special monkey was born from a magical rock on the Mountain of Flowers and Fruit. He was courageous and cunning, so the other monkeys honoured him as their king. Though he was superior to his peers, Monkey realised that one day he would die, just like any other mortal creature. Determined to overcome death, he travelled far and wide, searching for a way to live forever.

A spiritual master agreed to train him as a disciple. Monkey learned many magic arts, including cloud-travelling and seventy-two types of shape-shifting. He could transform the hairs of his body into objects or living beings, even into clones of himself. But Monkey became arrogant. He dived into the ocean and forced the Dragon King to hand over a fearsome weapon – a golden-banded fighting staff that could change its size, multiply itself, and fight according to the whim of its master.

Thus armed, Monkey went to Hell and bullied the officials there to wipe his name from the Book of Life and Death. He was now truly immortal.

In an attempt to manage this wild creature, the Jade Emperor invited Monkey to Heaven and gave him a rank among the gods. However, when Monkey realised he had only been given the title of Head of the Heavenly Stables, he decided to rebel. In his fury, Monkey stole a range of heavenly treasures, including the Peaches of Immortality and the Pills of Longevity, and he drank the Jade Emperor's royal wine. Then he fled.

An army of a hundred thousand celestial warriors tried their best to arrest Monkey, but he defeated them all. The ferocity of the battle shook the whole world, but no one was able to subdue Monkey until a three-eyed heavenly general arrived, who could see through all of his tricks. Desperate, Monkey transformed himself into a temple, with his eyes as windows and mouth as the door. Not sure what to do with his tail, he transformed it into a flagpole, but it was still recognisable.

'Got you!' the heavenly general laughed. His cover blown, Monkey was finally captured.

The gods tried to melt Monkey down in a heavenly furnace, but he escaped unharmed, though his eyes were reddened by the smoke. In revenge, Monkey transformed himself into a three-headed, six-armed monster and threatened to destroy the Heavenly Palace.

Luckily, the Buddha stepped in. 'I bet you that you cannot travel beyond the limits of my hand,' the Buddha proposed. 'If you win, you can be the Heavenly Emperor. If I win, you must do as I say.'

'I can travel tens of thousands of miles in just one somersault!' Monkey boasted. He leaped onto a cloud and disappeared beyond the horizon. After a long while, he reached what appeared to be the end of the world – there was nothing to be seen, apart from five gigantic pillars holding up the sky.

'This must be it. I won!' Monkey cheered. To convince the Buddha that he had indeed been there, he wrote the words 'Monkey Was Here' on the middle pillar and peed on it as proof.

When Monkey got back, the Buddha was really annoyed. 'You peed on my middle finger! And you have lousy handwriting.'

Thus Monkey knew that, however smart and capable he was, he would never be able to overcome the Buddha's mighty power.

Furthermore, as punishment, the Buddha
transformed his five fingers into an enormous
mountain and placed it on top of Monkey.
He was to be trapped there for the next five
hundred years.

The Buddha returned to Heaven, where the gods congratulated him for capturing Monkey. However, something else was on his mind.

'I have many precious scriptures in India for the world's people to study, so they can learn to coexist in peace,' the Buddha announced. 'Someone should go to India and bring back the scriptures. He must be honest, faithful and able to endure much hardship along the way. Who would go in search of this person for me?'

'I will,' Guanyin the goddess volunteered.

Guanyin decided to go to the Tang Empire, to see if one of the Emperor's many talented servants would be willing to go to India. However, when she arrived, she found that the Emperor was not in a state to be asked favours. He was troubled by visions. Every time he closed his eyes, he saw a headless dragon drenched in blood. The Emperor was concerned that this was a bad omen, and appointed a monk named Xuanzang

to lead the empire in praying for heavenly
blessings.

Although Xuanzang was only in his twenties,
he was known as a great scholar and religious
leader. He had also endured a difficult life. When
he was only a baby, a bandit had murdered his
father and kidnapped his mother. Fearing for her
son's life, Xuanzang's mother had hidden him in
a bush. Officials from a nearby temple had found
him and raised him as a monk.

Guanyin now revealed herself to the Emperor.
Thanks to her blessings and Xuanzang's prayers,
he ceased having visions.

Guanyin asked Xuanzang whether he would
accept the daunting task of travelling to India to
bring back the precious scriptures. Xuanzang
immediately said 'Yes', knowing that the wisdom
contained in the scriptures could enlighten his
fellow citizens on the important matters of peace
and life's values.

Guanyin gave Xuanzang a magical headband. 'Once you trick someone into putting on this headband, it can never be removed,' she instructed. 'With a special chant, the headband will tighten and cause unbearable pain to its wearer. Use it wisely to protect yourself.'

Xuanzang thanked the goddess, and began his journey to the west.

No sooner had Xuanzang crossed the empire's border than he realised how terribly difficult his journey would be. As he rested on a hilltop, rubbing his sore feet, he could see soaring mountains, wild rivers, dark forests and unpredictable lands stretching ahead. Lurking among these were bandits and beasts that might kill him, demons and monsters that might eat him alive.

But Xuanzang was determined to move on. Even when the locals warned him that there was a demon creeping around the nearby Five-Pillar Mountain, he was not afraid. Faith was his weapon.

The Five-Pillar Mountain had five peaks resembling gigantic fingers holding up the sky. Although Xuanzang was miles away, he could already hear a voice booming like thunder. 'Get me out! Get me out!'

When he reached the mountain, Xuanzang saw the most peculiar thing he had ever seen – a monkey was trapped under the foot of the middle peak, with only his head, shoulders and arms visible. Grass was growing out of his nostrils and ears. Moss covered his whole face. Yet the monkey was ecstatic.

'Finally someone's here! Get me out, and I'll do whatever you want,' he yelled.

'What are you?' Xuanzang asked. 'And why should I free you?'

'Because I am the greatest creature in the world!' Monkey rolled his eyes. 'Not even a whole army of celestial warriors could capture me!'

'So why are you trapped here?' Xuanzang smiled.

Embarrassed, Monkey only mumbled.

Xuanzang was a kind man. Besides, he could do with a bodyguard. 'If I were to help you, how could I lift the mountain?' he asked.

'Easy,' Monkey replied. 'Go to the mountaintop, where you will find a golden seal stuck on a rock. Peel it off, then run as far away as you can.'

Xuanzang did as Monkey had suggested. Immediately, the earth began to shake violently. Just as he was worried that the whole mountain would crumple to pieces, Monkey suddenly appeared in front of him. 'I'm free! To show you my gratitude, I'll honour you as my master!'

Monkey was an excellent disciple and bodyguard, finding food and accommodation and fending off all attackers, bandits and beasts alike. However, Xuanzang was concerned about his aggressive nature.

'You only need to scare them off,' Xuanzang scolded. 'As a monk's disciple, you should never commit the crime of killing.'

'I'll do whatever I want,' Monkey retorted. 'If you irritate me, I'll kill you too!'

Xuanzang knew he had to protect himself. 'I have something nice for a great warrior like you,' he smiled, showing Monkey the magical headband Guanyin had given him.

Monkey was so delighted that he immediately put it on.

As soon as Xuanzang started reciting the special chant Guanyin had taught him, Monkey felt as if someone was squeezing his head. The pain was unbearable. He tried to smash the headband into pieces with his golden-banded fighting staff; then he tried to ease the pain by doing somersaults and standing on his head. Nothing worked.

Finally he begged, 'Please, Master! Stop that chanting!'

'Will you obey me now?' Xuanzang demanded.

'Yes, yes! I'll do whatever you want!' Monkey shrieked. From then on, he swore, he would never misbehave again.

When Xuanzang and Monkey stopped at a village for food, the locals warned them that a monster had been disguising itself as a man to seduce innocent girls. 'I'll capture the monster for you,' Monkey promised.

Monkey transformed himself into a beautiful village girl. When the monster came and tried to grab her, Monkey gave him a good beating and forced him to surrender. Xuanzang accepted the monster as his second disciple, naming him Piggy. In his former life, Piggy had been a heavenly marshal in command of eighty thousand troops. At a gathering in Heaven, he became drunk and tried to seduce the Goddess of Moon, and as punishment was banished to the world. In his fall from Heaven, he fell into a barn and was reborn as a pig with an unquenchable appetite.

Piggy wielded a nine-tooth rake as a weapon, and knew thirty-six types of shape-shifting. He considered himself as good a warrior as Monkey, and could not stop grumbling when given the job of carrying the luggage. Worse, now that Piggy had become the disciple of a monk, he could no longer eat meat nor drink wine.

At their next stop, by the Flowing-Sand River, Xuanzang was captured by a monster wearing a necklace of nine human skulls. Knowing that Piggy was better at fighting under water than he was, Monkey asked him to tackle the monster and rescue Xuanzang.

But even Piggy could not conquer the monster, so Monkey went to Heaven and asked Guanyin for help. She succeeded in subduing the monster and even persuaded him to become Xuanzang's third disciple. He was given the name Sandy, after the river. Guanyin transformed Sandy's nine skulls into a boat that carried Xuanzang across the river.

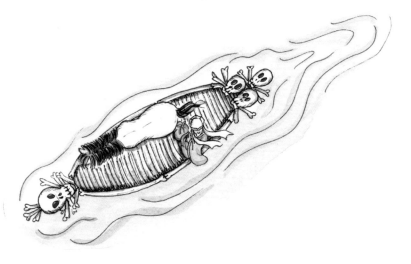

Sandy had formerly been a heavenly general. Having accidentally smashed the Jade Emperor's vase, he was banished to the world and reborn as a water monster. Sandy knew eighteen types of shape-shifting. His weapon was a double-headed staff with a crescent-moon blade at one end and a shovel at the other.

Xuanzang and his disciples continued their journey towards India. They decided to rest at a spiritual master's residence, where there grew an amazing tree that produced fruit only once every ten thousand years. These magical fruit looked very much like human babies, yet those fortunate enough to taste them would be free of illness throughout their lives.

When the spiritual master presented Xuanzang with one of the baby-shaped fruits as a gift, he refused to eat it. Monkey was less squeamish. Indeed, when he realised he was not going to be offered the fruit, he was so upset

that he uprooted the tree. Immediately, all the magical fruit disappeared underground.

The spiritual master was very angry at the loss of his tree, and imprisoned Xuanzang and his disciples. Monkey was now full of regret for what he had done, and begged the spiritual master not to punish Xuanzang. He escaped to Heaven to seek help from their friend and helper, Guanyin.

Guanyin was able to bring the tree back to life, using water from her Vase of Purity. The tree regained its magical fruit, and now Xuanzang ate one, recognising it as something precious. Monkey, Piggy and Sandy each received a piece too. Then the four of them bade farewell to the spiritual master and continued their journey.

The travellers journeyed onwards. After many miles they began to feel very hungry. They came upon a beautiful girl who offered them some food. Xuanzang, Piggy and Sandy believed in her kindness, but Monkey was sure it was a trick and attacked her. Monkey was correct in his guess – though none of them knew it, the beautiful girl was actually a demon in disguise to fool them. The demon escaped from Monkey, leaving behind its shell, which resembled a female human corpse.

'Such an innocent girl, and you killed her!' Piggy complained.

Xuanzang was upset, but thought that Monkey knew what he was doing. However, the demon continued disguising itself as different people. Each time, after being attacked by Monkey, the demon left behind a different 'corpse'. Finally, Xuanzang began to believe Piggy's accusation that Monkey was truly of a murderous nature.

'Go away!' Xuanzang yelled at Monkey. 'I don't want you as my disciple any more. You've done enough!'

'Yes, Monkey's violent behaviour will only put us in danger,' Piggy encouraged.

'Master, please!' Monkey begged, on his knees.
'Who's going to protect you if I leave?'

'Piggy and Sandy will,' Xuanzang demanded.
'Now go, or I'll recite that special chant!'

Knowing that there was nothing he could say
or do to change Xuanzang's mind, Monkey left. He
went back to the Mountain of Flowers and Fruit,
and resumed his leadership of the monkeys.

One evening Piggy went searching for food and left
Sandy with Xuanzang. Having filled his stomach,
he forgot about the two waiting for him and fell
asleep under a tree. Xuanzang was worried that
Piggy might have got lost, and sent Sandy to
find him. Now completely alone and vulnerable,

Xuanzang was captured by a monster, who took him to its cave.

Meanwhile Sandy had found the lazy Piggy, and together they had gone looking for Xuanzang. They searched every cave and river in the nearby mountains, and finally came to the monster's cave.

'Halt!' Piggy and Sandy shouted at the monster, who was just about to start cooking Xuanzang in a pot. As the pair fought the monster, Piggy became scared that he too could become a delicious meal. He ran away, leaving Sandy behind, but Sandy was no match for the monster.

With both Xuanzang and Sandy captured, Piggy realised that only Monkey could help them. He travelled to the Mountain of Flowers and Fruit and begged Monkey to come back.

'I'm the king here, free to do whatever I want. Why should I go and serve that monk who wouldn't even trust me?' Monkey grumbled.

'You have to save Master. He's been captured by a monster who thinks you're an idiot,' Piggy lied. 'The monster told me that if you dare to bother him, he'll peel off your skin, pull out your bones, and stir-fry you in oil. He has absolutely no respect for you.'

Monkey jumped up, furious. 'Who does this monster think he is? I'll teach him a lesson!'

Monkey fought and defeated the monster. He then set Xuanzang and Sandy free, who were still shaking after their terrible experience.

'From now on,' Xuanzang gratefully said to Monkey, 'I'll never doubt you again.'

As they continued on their travels, Xuanzang and his disciples met a boy wearing a red shirt who seemed lost. While Xuanzang wanted to help the boy find his parents, Monkey recognised him as a demon.

'We're coming to help you,' Piggy and Sandy yelled, pulling out their weapons.

'No, stay with Master!' Monkey warned them.

But it was too late. The boy suddenly transformed himself into a great red tornado and swept Xuanzang away.

The local god of land told Monkey, Piggy and Sandy that the demon was the Red Boy, son of Buffalo King and Princess Iron-Fan. The three of them fought the demon, but were defeated by his magical fire and smoke. Piggy ran away, fearing that he would turn into a roast pig, and Monkey and Sandy were both badly burned. Even after Monkey asked the Dragon King for help, the rain falling from Heaven could not overpower the Red Boy's fire.

Again, Monkey went to Heaven to ask for Guanyin's help, and again she came to their aid. She poured water out of her Vase of Purity and smothered the Red Boy's fire. Unashamed, the demon attacked Guanyin and snatched her throne, which was made of a thousand lotus flowers. He sat on it proudly,

pleased with his defeat of the goddess. But
Guanyin transformed the lotus flowers into a
thousand sharp knives and trapped him.

The Red Boy now agreed to surrender and
to become Guanyin's disciple. However, the
goddess was still concerned that he might rebel,
so she transformed a magical headband into five
and put them on the Red Boy's head, wrists and
ankles.

'Don't you recite that special chant and hurt me,' Monkey panicked. 'Haven't I been good all this time?'

'Relax, Monkey,' Guanyin smiled. 'This headband and chant are just for him.' She took the Red Boy back to Heaven, and Monkey, Piggy and Sandy were reunited with their master.

As they continued on their travels, Xuanzang and his disciples noticed a huge crowd of monks working by the roadside. Two guards were giving orders. As the travellers watched, some of the monks fell and were severely beaten. Others wept bitterly.

Upset by such cruelty, Monkey asked the monks about their situation. The monks explained that they had been enslaved by three priests, Tigery, Deery and Goaty, who used their magical powers to serve the king from the nearby kingdom. These priests had promised to make the king live forever, so he favoured them and despised the monks, accusing them of chanting all day and doing nothing practical.

'I'll seek justice for you,' Monkey promised. He pulled off a handful of his body hairs and gave one to each monk. 'Hold it in your hand. If anyone bothers you, just say my name and I'll be there to protect you.' The monks happily walked away, knowing that hundreds of Monkey's clones would look after them.

Next, Monkey, Piggy and Sandy disguised themselves as statues of gods in the kingdom's largest temple. When the priests Tigery, Deery and Goaty came to pray, they found that all the people's offerings had been consumed, and in their place was a bowl of holy water. 'It tastes a bit salty,' Tigery said.

'That's because it's our pee!' Monkey, Piggy and Sandy burst out laughing as they changed back to their normal selves. To convince the king that these priests were actually deceitful demons, Monkey challenged them in three magical tests.

Priest Tigery claimed that he could manipulate the weather. 'I don't believe you!' Monkey snorted. He secretly ordered the gods in charge of wind, clouds, thunder, lightning and rain not to obey the priest's orders. Thus Priest Tigery failed the first test and was executed by the king. As the axe fell, he resumed his true form, which was a wild tiger.

Priest Deery claimed that he could stay alive with his head chopped off.

'What a joke!' Monkey sneered. When the priest's head was removed, Monkey pulled off one of his own body hairs and transformed it into a dog, which snatched the priest's head and ran away with it. Deery died and resumed his true form as a wild deer.

Priest Goaty vowed to avenge his two friends. He claimed that he could bathe in boiling oil, and challenged Monkey to do the same.

'Easy!' Monkey jumped into a pot of boiling oil and happily splashed around.

He then discovered that Goaty, in his bath, had lowered the oil's temperature by magic. Monkey quickly brought the oil back to boiling point. Thus Goaty was scalded to death. In dying, he returned to his true form of a wild goat.

Monkey warned the king not to trust demons again.

One day, while crossing a beautiful river, Xuanzang and Piggy drank of its water to ease their thirst. Later that day the four travellers arrived at a kingdom whose citizens were all women. Piggy felt very happy.

However, as soon as they found accommodation at a local inn, Xuanzang and Piggy began to develop severe stomach aches, their bellies swelling up as if something was growing inside.

'Ah, you drank from the Mother River, didn't you?' the female innkeeper grinned. 'Congratulations! You'll have a baby soon!'

'How can a man give birth to a baby?' Piggy was terrified.

'Maybe the baby will drill its way out of your armpit!' Monkey teased, ignoring Xuanzang's alarmed protests.

However, the local people told them of a cure. Monkey and Sandy found a spring whose water, it was said, could dissolve the foetuses growing inside Xuanzang's and Piggy's bellies. And indeed, as soon as Xuanzang and Piggy drank the water fetched from the spring, they felt normal again.

Trembling, the four travellers left the kingdom of women as fast as they could.

Further along the road to India, bandits attacked the travellers. Monkey quickly disposed of them all. Xuanzang was very upset that this disciple had killed again, and repeated the special chant that tightened Monkey's headband. Monkey went to Heaven and begged Guanyin to remove the magical headband.

'My master doesn't want me any more. Why can't you take this thing off me and set me free?' Monkey complained.

'You shouldn't have committed the crime of killing,' Guanyin scolded. 'Besides, your master will be in trouble soon. Just wait until he needs you.'

Xuanzang sent Piggy and Sandy to search for water and food. As he waited by the roadside, Monkey suddenly appeared with a cup of water.

'See, you can't do without me,' Monkey boasted.

'Go away!' Xuanzang yelled, still angry. 'I'd rather die than drink your water!'

'You stupid monk, how dare you treat me like trash!' Monkey kicked Xuanzang to the ground, grabbed his luggage, and disappeared.

When Piggy and Sandy came back and found Xuanzang, faint and bruised all over, they became seriously annoyed.

'You look after Master and I'll go and beat up that beastly monkey!' Piggy shrieked.

'Let's find Master some food and a place to rest first,' Sandy suggested.

After they had found a place to stay for the night, Sandy volunteered to find Monkey and bring back Xuanzang's luggage. When he arrived at the Mountain of Flowers and Fruit, he was shocked to find that Monkey was getting ready to travel to India and bring back the precious scriptures by himself. There were even a Xuanzang, a Piggy and a Sandy there – fake ones that Monkey had produced magically out of his fellow monkeys.

Even in his fury Sandy knew that he should not confront Monkey and risk getting killed. Instead, he travelled to Heaven to seek Guanyin's advice. On his arrival he was shocked to find Monkey there too.

'You wretched monkey, I'll kill you this time!' Sandy dashed forward, shouting and pulling out his double-headed staff.

'Halt!' Guanyin demanded. 'What's going on here?'

Sandy described all the wrongs Monkey had done, but the goddess shook her head. 'Monkey's innocent, for he's been with me all this time,' Guanyin considered. 'It must be someone else who stole the luggage and created false versions of Xuanzang, Piggy and you.'

Monkey and Sandy returned to the Mountain of Flowers and Fruit and found the other Monkey there.

'I'm the real Monkey. Who are you?' Monkey waved his fists.

'*I'm* the real Monkey. Who are *you*?' the other Monkey rolled his eyes.

While Sandy brought the luggage back to Xuanzang and Piggy, the two Monkeys returned to Heaven to seek justice, kicking and screaming at each other along the way. However, none of the gods could tell the difference between them.

Guanyin recited her special chant, only to see both Monkeys jumping up and down, begging her to stop. Even the Jade Emperor's demon-exposing mirror could not reveal which one was the false Monkey.

Eventually, the two Monkeys were brought to the Buddha. Showing the same mighty power that had subdued Monkey five hundred years ago, he needed only to look at them. Immediately, the pretender, a six-eared monkey that was nearly but not quite as magical as Monkey, surrendered.

The Buddha blessed the real Monkey, who returned to join Xuanzang, Piggy and Sandy on their way to India.

As Xuanzang and his disciples travelled onward, every day became hotter, even though it was winter. The locals warned them that they were near the Mountain of Flames, whose radiant heat could destroy anything within eight hundred miles. To survive here, one had to get Princess Iron-Fan to use her magical fan to calm the flames and bring wind and rain.

'Uh-oh, Princess Iron-Fan is mother of the Red Boy,' Monkey reminded Xuanzang, Piggy and Sandy. 'How will we get her to use her fan to help us?'

Indeed, when Monkey visited Princess Iron-Fan, he found her extremely angry about what had happened to her son. She sent Monkey flying with a wave of her magical fan. By the time he finally landed on his feet, he had drifted tens of thousands of miles away.

Monkey was determined to get hold of the fan. He returned to Princess Iron-Fan's palace, transformed himself into a bug, and dived into her cup of tea. When she sipped her tea, he landed inside her stomach where he started doing cartwheels and somersaults.

'Ok, ok, I'll give you the fan!' Princess Iron-Fan moaned in pain. 'Now would you just come out of me!'

Monkey was so happy with the fan that he used it on the mountain right away. However, instead of calming the flames, the fan caused them to grow miles high; now they threatened to consume everything within sight.

Monkey managed to escape the flames, his skin singed and smelling of smoke. 'That deceitful demon gave me a false fan!' he cursed.

The local God of Land told Monkey that Princess Iron-Fan's husband, Buffalo King, also had magical powers. Monkey decided that if he could capture Buffalo King, then Princess Iron-Fan would have to surrender her fan.

Monkey challenged Buffalo King. The two of them fought bitterly, but neither could defeat the other. Both combatants enlarged themselves a thousand times. All the spectators could see was an enormous buffalo confronting a gigantic monkey.

Piggy and Sandy joined the battle. Although they managed to cut off Buffalo King's head several times, he kept growing it back, each time becoming stronger.

Finally, Monkey went to Heaven and
borrowed the Jade Emperor's demon-exposing
mirror. As Buffalo King's reflection appeared
in the mirror, the real him was trapped. He
admitted defeat and asked Princess Iron-Fan to
hand over her magical fan.

Monkey waved the fan at the mountain forty-
nine times and succeeded in smothering the
flames forever. Now all the people living nearby
could enjoy cool and happy lives.

As Xuanzang and his disciples neared India, they needed to pass through a series of small kingdoms. In the first kingdom, they were warned that the king had vowed to kill ten thousand monks. Since nine thousand, nine hundred and ninety-six monks had already died, Xuanzang was in danger of being the ten thousandth. The four of them were now in great peril.

Monkey pulled off all the hairs on his right arm and transformed them into thousands of tiny clones of himself. He then removed all the hairs on his left arm, turned them into thousands of sleep-inducing bugs and spread them throughout the palace. While everybody in the palace, from the king and queen to the officials and soldiers, slept, Monkey transformed his golden-banded fighting staff into thousands of razors and gave one to each of his clones. These tiny Monkeys shaved everyone in the palace and turned them all into monks.

45

When the king woke up in the morning and discovered that everyone in his palace was now a monk, including himself, he rethought his policy of killing monks. He promised to mend his ways and lead his kingdom in promoting peace.

The next kingdom they entered had not seen rain for three years. When Xuanzang asked Monkey to beg the Dragon King for rain, they were told that the drought was ordered by the Jade Emperor himself. Monkey went straight to Heaven and demanded an explanation.

'Three years ago the ruler of the kingdom was disrespectful to me,' the Jade Emperor answered. 'He spilled the offerings that had been left in a temple dedicated to me and then fed them to dogs. It was a great sacrilege, so I decided to punish him.'

The Jade Emperor showed Monkey three things. The first was an enormous pile of rice, with a chick pecking from it. The second was a huge mountain of flour, with a puppy licking from it. The third was

a bar of gold as thick as one's thumb, with a tiny
candle flame burning under it.

'Only after the chick has consumed all the
rice, the puppy has licked up all the flour, and the
candle flame has burned through the bar of gold,
will I agree to bring rain to the kingdom,' the Jade
Emperor announced. 'Don't you try to interfere,
Monkey. I won't change my mind.'

Monkey returned to the kingdom of drought, and told the king what the Jade Emperor had said.

'It's all my fault,' the king confessed. 'Three years ago, in that temple, I had a fight with my queen. In my fury I kicked the altar and spilled all the offerings, which were later eaten by my dogs. I deserve to be punished, but my people are innocent! Please help us!'

Monkey advised the king to lead his people in praying for heavenly blessings. An altar was set up in every household and offerings were made. Every man, woman and child bathed themselves and pleaded that Heaven forgive their sins, vowing that from now on they would strive to improve themselves and each other. The king knelt in front of his palace for days to show his remorse.

The Jade Emperor forgave them. In Heaven, the mountains of rice and flour suddenly vanished, and the bar of gold broke in half. In the sky above the kingdom, the gods in charge of wind, clouds, thunder, lightning and rain arrived to produce a great rainstorm that quenched the earth's thirst. The king and his people knelt on the ground to express their gratitude towards Heaven. Then everyone danced in joy, completely soaked.

The last kingdom before India had a beautiful princess who was planning to get married. From her balcony, she would throw a ball made of coloured silk at the man she thought would make an ideal husband. By the time Xuanzang and his disciples arrived, large crowds of men had already gathered in front of the palace.

Xuanzang only wanted to pay a brief visit to the king, but as the would-be suitors jostled each other, eager to show off their looks and talents, the princess threw her ball straight at Xuanzang. It bounced off his head and landed in his hands.

'The princess has chosen a monk as husband!' The crowds cheered.

'Not again!' Xuanzang panicked as the royal

servants carried him into the palace. 'I've got work to do! I'm not getting married!'

'Relax, Master,' Monkey smiled. 'I'll handle this.'

Monkey discovered that the so-called princess was not really human, and attacked her. She fought back, using a pestle-shaped weapon. As they battled, the Goddess of Moon arrived in search of her rabbit that had sneaked out of the Moon Palace.

'There you are!' the goddess scolded the princess, who immediately resumed her true self as a rabbit. 'Since you left, no one's been able to make medicine for me. I can't even use the mortar to grind herbs and spices, for you've stolen the pestle!'

The Goddess of Moon found the real princess and returned her to the palace. Now the goddess was ready to leave with her rabbit, but Piggy grabbed her. 'Do you miss me?' he leered, remembering that once, when drunk, he had tried to seduce her. 'I'm a monk now!'

'Behave yourself, or I'll ask Monkey to give you a good beating,' Xuanzang scolded. Piggy lowered his head in shame.

At last, fourteen years after Xuanzang left the Tang Empire, the party arrived in India. Here were gentle hills covered with green trees and brilliant flowers. The people were civilised and deeply religious, and greeted them warmly.

'So this is where the precious scriptures are kept,' Xuanzang smiled, remembering the numerous obstacles he and his three disciples had encountered on their way. All those bandits, beasts, demons and monsters were tests he had to face in order to prove his determination to reach India. Now he had finally achieved his goal.

On top of the tallest hill, the Buddha greeted them with the precious scriptures. 'Contained in these scriptures is wisdom that will help people of this world evade all miseries and be enlightened about life. Take them back with you, and do your best to pass them on.'

The Buddha asked the gods to carry Xuanzang and his disciples back to the Tang Empire. As soon as they had presented the precious scriptures to the Tang Emperor, they were to come back to India and be rewarded for their hard work.

The journey back to the east flashed in front of their eyes as the gods carried them on the wind. The Emperor was very pleased to see that Xuanzang had returned safely with the precious scriptures. He was also delighted to know that Xuanzang had acquired three talented disciples.

The Emperor ordered that the precious scriptures be displayed in a special temple dedicated to the Buddha, available for all citizens to worship and study. A huge party was held, both to celebrate Xuanzang's return and to thank Heaven's blessings.

However, Xuanzang and his disciples had to leave again. It would be their last journey to the west.

The Buddha greeted the four travellers. He revealed that Xuanzang had once been a god, but had been banished to the world as punishment for disrespecting heavenly rules. Xuanzang would now become the Glorious Sandalwood Buddha as a reward for his honesty, faith and determination.

Meanwhile, Monkey would become the Buddha of Conquest as a reward for his dedication, courage and ingenuity.

As a reward for his persistence and lack of pretence, Piggy, who had always enjoyed food and wine, would become the Cleanser of the Heavenly Altar and receive all excess offerings.

Sandy would become the Golden-Bodied God as a reward for his loyalty and patience.

Thus the four of them remained among the gods in Heaven. However, Monkey was still not happy. 'Can you now remove this ghastly headband?' he complained to Xuanzang. 'As soon as I get hold of it, I'm going to smash it into a thousand pieces!'

'Now you've become a god, how can the headband still be there?' Xuanzang smiled.

Monkey reached for his headband. It was indeed gone.

TAKING THINGS FURTHER

The real read

This *Real Read* version of *Journey to the West* is a retelling in English of Wu Cheng'en's magnificent Chinese work. If you would like to read the full Chinese novel in all its original splendour, you will need to learn the Chinese language. Otherwise, you will have to rely on various English translations of the novel.

Filling in the spaces

The loss of so many of Wu Cheng'en's original words is a sad but necessary part of the shortening process. We have had to make some difficult decisions, omitting subplots and characters, some important, some less so, but all interesting. We have also, at times, taken the liberty of combining two events into one, or of giving a character words or actions that originally belonged to another. The points below will fill in some of the gaps, but nothing can beat the original.

- Wu Cheng'en's *Journey to the West* provides much more detailed description about Monkey's birth, study of magical arts, and adventures around the world before he became Xuanzang's disciple. There are also more words on Monkey's battles against all kinds of heavenly generals and soldiers, before he is subdued by the Buddha.

- Wu devotes many pages to describing the early part of Xuanzang's life and the background of his journey to the west. For example, Xuanzang is eventually able to reunite with his mother. It is through Xuanzang's maternal grandfather, a high-ranking government official, that he meets the Emperor, who has previously had a near-death experience and is now praying for heavenly blessings.

- In Wu's *Journey to the West*, Xuanzang encounters far more demons and monsters who regard him as a potential meal. There are also goblins and ogres, many of whom turn out to be the earthly manifestations of heavenly beings (whose sins will be negated by eating the monk), and animal-spirits, who have gained enough spiritual merit to assume semi-human forms.

- In Wu's *Journey to the West*, Monkey, Piggy and Sandy have all had previous dealings with Guanyin the Goddess. She tells them to wait for the arrival of a 'scripture seeker', and their duty will be to serve him throughout his journey to the west. This is why Monkey, Piggy and Sandy are so easily persuaded to become Xuanzang's disciples – they know already that it is their call of duty.

- In Wu's *Journey to the West*, Xuanzang's fourth disciple is his horse, who is actually the third prince of the Dragon King. Guanyin saves him from death and lets him serve the monk, which he does dutifully.

- Some of the obstacles encountered by Xuanzang and his disciples are engineered by the Buddha as a test of their willingness to complete the journey. Near the end of Wu's *Journey to the West*, there is even a scene where the Buddha actually commands disasters to happen.

Back in time

Wu Cheng'en wrote *Journey to the West* in the 1590s. The Chinese government at that time was not very efficient, unable to protect its citizens against natural disasters and widespread turmoil caused by rebels, bandits and pirates. It must have been a sad time to live in, especially for Wu, who failed the national examination and thus lost the opportunity to become a government official and look after his fellow people.

Wu based his book on the legends of a Chinese monk named Xuanzang who, in the seventh century, travelled to India and spent thirteen years studying Buddhism there. After returning to China, he dedicated his life to translating and teaching the Buddhist scriptures he had brought back.

Throughout Chinese history there have been many popular stories and folk tales about Xuanzang's achievement. During his writing of *Journey to the West*, Wu was heavily influenced by these stories and tales, which have a strong background in Chinese folk beliefs, myths and value systems.

More importantly, the book was written in 'vernacular' Chinese, which is the language used by ordinary people in their daily lives, as opposed to the jargon and specialised terminology used by experts and academics. This is why *Journey to the West* is considered one of the most popular Chinese novels of all time – it contains a lot of humour, satire, emotional and physical conflicts, and symbols and allegories that are well known to ordinary Chinese readers.

Journey to the West is very much about the character Monkey and his transformation from a mischievous magical creature to a supernatural hero. Unlike Xuanzang, Piggy and Sandy, who have committed sins in their previous lives and are thus banished to the human world to redeem their faults, Monkey was born magically out of a rock and therefore has no previous life. His courage to accept and pay for the mistakes he has made, by devoting his life to protecting Xuanzang throughout their journey, is considered worthy of respect.

Some Chinese scholars suggest that the many demons and monsters encountered by Xuanzang and his disciples in their journey represent various aspects of the dark side of their personalities. The fact that these evil creatures either try to obtain immortality by eating the monk's flesh, or are attracted to his good looks, suggests the author's attempt to promote the importance of inner beauty. What are the values of flesh and blood, he is asking, if a person does not have a true heart?

Finding out more

We recommend the following English books and websites to gain a greater understanding of Wu Cheng'en and his novel:

Books

- Arthur Waley (translator), *Monkey: Folk Novel of China*, Evergreen Books, 1994. An abridged translation of the Chinese novel.

- W.J.F. Jenner (translator), *Journey to the West*, Foreign Language Press, Beijing, 2003. A complete translation of the Chinese novel in four volumes.

- James S. Fu, *Mythic and Comic Aspects of the Quest*, Singapore University Press, 1977.

- Andrew Plaks, *The Four Masterworks of the Ming Novel*, Princeton University Press, 1987.

- Barbara S. Miller (editor), *Masterworks of Asian Literature in Comparative Perspective*, M.E. Sharpe, 1993.

Websites

- www.china-on-site.com/pages/comic/1.php
A series of traditional-style Chinese paintings portraying the story of Monkey and the beginning of *Journey to the West*.

- en.wikipedia.org/wiki/Journey_to_the_west
The Wikipedia page on *Journey to the West*, with links to other pages about the novel's author and main characters.

- www.pantheon.org/articles/s/sun_wu-kung.html
Monkey's profile at Encyclopedia Mythica.

- www.vbtutor.net/Xiyouji/psunwukong.htm
A detailed character profile of Monkey, with details
of his various names and titles, information about
his weapons, abilities, powers and skills, and
explanations of his personality.

Food for thought

Here are some things to think about if you are
reading *Journey to the West* alone, or ideas for
discussion if you are reading it with friends.

In retelling *Journey to the West* we have tried to
recreate, as accurately as possible, Wu Cheng'en's
original plot and characters. We have also tried to
imitate aspects of his style. Remember, however,
that this is not the original work; thinking about
the points below, therefore, can help you begin to
understand Wu Cheng'en's craft. To move forward
from here, turn to the abridged or full-length
English translations of *Journey to the West* and lose
yourself in his wonderful storytelling.

Starting points

- Which character interests you the most? Why?

- What do you think of Monkey? Do your feelings towards him change as you read on? How?

- Monkey uses his magical powers to solve all kinds of problems. Which is more important – the means, or the results?

- Not everybody has magical powers. If Wu Cheng'en was writing today, what technologies might he include to help Xuanzang and his disciples complete their journey from China to India?

Themes

What do you think Wu Cheng'en is saying about the following themes in *Journey to the West*?

- loyalty

- honesty

- determination

- courage

- faith

Style

Can you find paragraphs containing examples of the following?

- humour

- satire

- a character exposing his true character through something he says or the way he speaks

Look closely at how these paragraphs are written. What do you notice? Can you write a paragraph in the same style?